This book belongs to...

British Library Cataloguing in Publication Data

A catalogue record for this book is
available from the British Library

ISBN 0 340 87375 2(HB)

Text and illustrations copyright © Mick Inkpen 1990, 1987, 1997

The right of Mick Inkpen to be identified as the author
of this Work has been asserted by him in accordance with
the Copyright, Designs and Patents Act 1988.

Threadbear first published 1990
One Bear at Bedtime first published 1987
Bear first published 1997

First published 2002 by
Hodder Children's Books,
a division of Hodder Headline Limited,
338 Euston Road, London NW1 3BH

This edition produced for the Book People Ltd
Hall Wood Avenue, Haydock, St Helens WA11 9UL

10 9 8 7 6 5 4 3 2 1

Printed in Hong Kong

Mick Inkpen
Bear Stories

Threadbear • One Bear at Bedtime • Bear

TED SMART

Threadbear

Ben's bear was called Threadbear. He was old. Bits of him had worn out. Or worked loose. Or dropped off.

He had a paw which didn't match, and a button for an eye. When he looked through the button he saw four pictures instead of one. It was like looking in a television shop window.

But there was one thing that had always been wrong with Threadbear. The silly man who had made him had put too much stuffing inside him. His arms were too hard. His legs were too hard. And there was so much stuffing inside his tummy that his squeaker had been squashed. It had never squeaked. Not even once.

Threadbear hated having a squeaker in his tummy that wouldn't squeak. It made him feel that he was letting Ben down.

Ben's frog could croak. His space monster could squelch. And his electronic robot could burble away for hours if its batteries were the right way round.

Even the little toy that Ben called Grey Thing could make a noise, and nobody knew what Grey Thing was meant to be!

Nobody could make Threadbear's squeaker work.

Ben's dad couldn't do it.

His mum couldn't do it.

Nor could his auntie or his grandma.

Nor could any
of his friends.

When Ben had measles he asked the doctor about Threadbear's squeaker.

The doctor listened to Threadbear's tummy. But there was no squeak. Not even the faintest sign of one.

The other toys tried to help.

'If you had a winder like me, we could wind you up,' said Frog.

'If you were made of rubber like me, we could squelch you,' said the space monster.

'If you had batteries like me, we could turn you on,' said the robot. It was not much help.

'Why don't you ask Father Christmas?' said Grey Thing. 'He knows all about toys.'

This was a brilliant idea and Grey Thing went a little pink.

'But where does Father Christmas live?' asked Threadbear.

'At a place called the North Pole,' said Grey Thing. 'You can get to it up the chimney I think.'

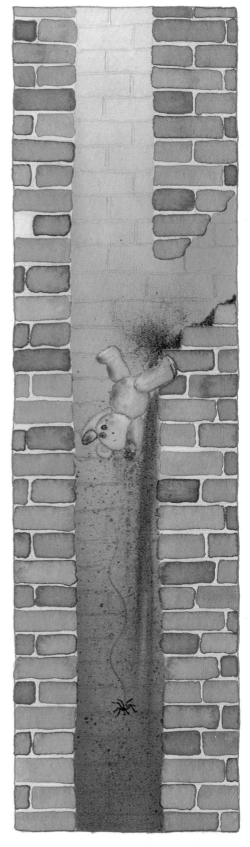

Threadbear had never climbed up a chimney before. It was hard work. He took a wrong turn and fell back down. But he did not give up.

It was long after bedtime when Threadbear poked his head out of the chimney pot.

This must be the North Pole!

Threadbear sat down to wait for Father
Christmas. He waited and waited. But Father
Christmas did not seem to be coming.
The moon rose into the sky and
Threadbear began to doze...

Suddenly Father Christmas was there
helping Threadbear into his sleigh!

Threadbear felt himself
falling and falling...

Threadbear could hear the squeaker
trees as they came in to land.

'You must eat the biggest squeaker fruit,'
said Father Christmas.

It tasted delicious but it made
Threadbear feel sleepy.

They flew over the top of the world and on
to the land where the squeaker trees grow.

Bump! Threadbear woke up. He rubbed his eyes and looked around. There was no squeaker fruit, no squeaker tree and worst of all no Father Christmas.

'I must have fallen asleep and dropped off the North Pole!' said Threadbear.

In the morning Ben was surprised to find Threadbear in the garden covered with soot. Ben's mum put Threadbear straight into the washing machine. She did not even look at the label on Threadbear's neck which read in capital letters DO NOT WASH!

When Threadbear came out of the washing machine the soot was gone, but there was a curious purple stain on his chin, which nobody could explain. Threadbear was feeling too giddy to notice. His head felt like a spinning top!

'I don't mind feeling giddy,' thought
Threadbear as he hung on the line.
'I don't mind having a button for an
eye and a paw that doesn't match.
I don't even mind being hung up by the
ear. But what I DO mind, what I mind
VERY MUCH is having a silly
squeaker in my tummy
that won't SQUEAK!'

Threadbear was so cross that he
frightened a robin. It flew away leaving
him alone in the garden bouncing angry
little bounces on the washing line.

The sun rose slowly over the garden.
It shone straight down on Threadbear,
a great warm shine like an enormous hug.
Threadbear began to steam. He began to
feel better. The more he steamed the
better he felt.

He swung his legs backwards and
forwards. Then he kicked them high in the
air. Soon he was swinging round and round
the washing line giggling to himself.

'Why do I feel so happy?' he wondered.

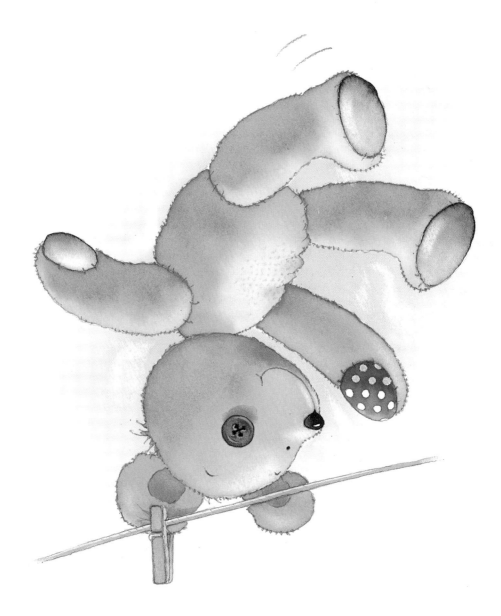

It was at this moment that Threadbear realised a very odd thing had happened to him. His paws felt different. So did his arms and his legs. They were no longer hard!

And inside his tummy was a wonderful, loose, comfortable feeling that he had never felt before!

At the very same moment something caught Threadbear's eye. Something red was racing across the sun. And to Threadbear's surprise the red something was waving goodbye!

When Ben came out to see
if Threadbear was dry he
noticed that his little brown
bear had changed.
'Look mum,' said Ben,
'He's gone floppy!'
Ben's mum unpegged
Threadbear's ear. 'Oh dear!' she said,
'His stuffing must have shrunk in the wash!'
Ben looked at Threadbear. 'I like him
like that. It makes him look...' But Ben
could not think of the right word so instead
he gave Threadbear a squeeze.
And for the first time the squeaker
in Threadbear's tummy gave the
loudest,
clearest,
squeakiest...

. . . squeak!

One Bear
At Bedtime

1

One bear at bedtime
is all I need...

2

I have two pigs
who wear my clothes…

3

Three kangaroos
who bounce on my bed…

4

Four giraffes
who sit in the bath…

5

Five lions who
mess about with
the shampoo…

6

Six snakes who
unwind the toilet roll…

7

Seven ostriches
who drink my milk…

8

Eight crocodiles
who use up all the
toothpaste…

9

Nine caterpillars
who crawl about at night...
(Did you spot them?)

10

And a monster
with ten heads
who takes forever
to say goodnight.

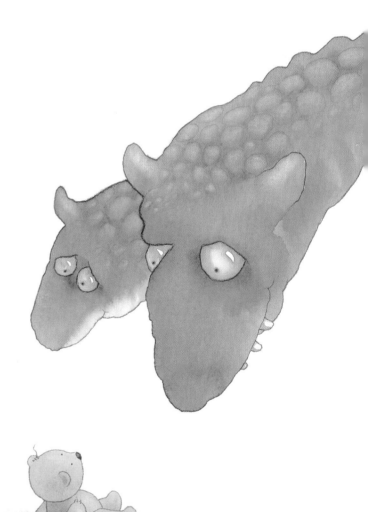

But one bear at bedtime…

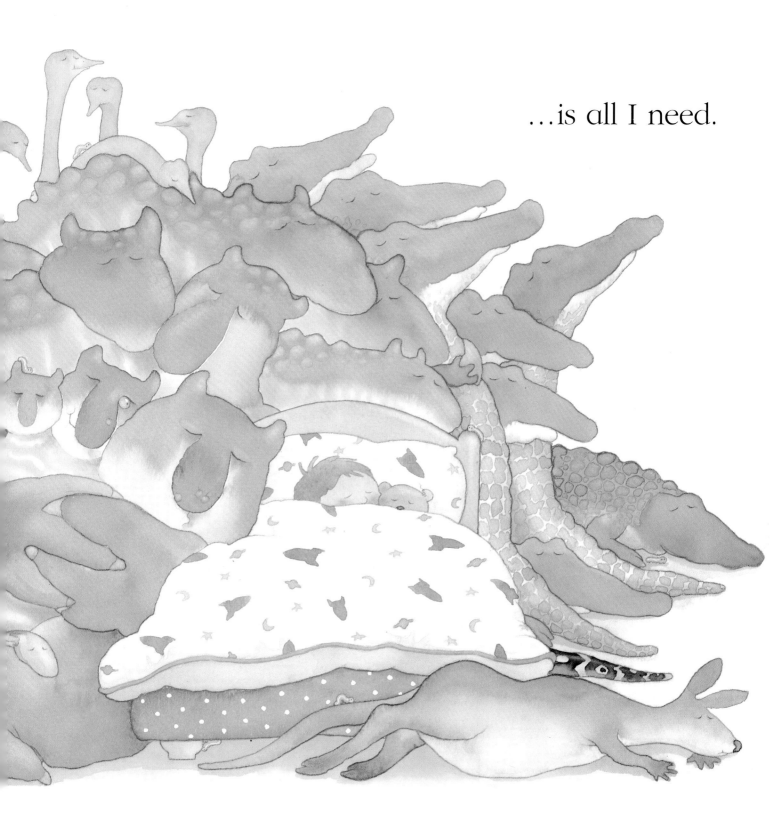

...is all I need.

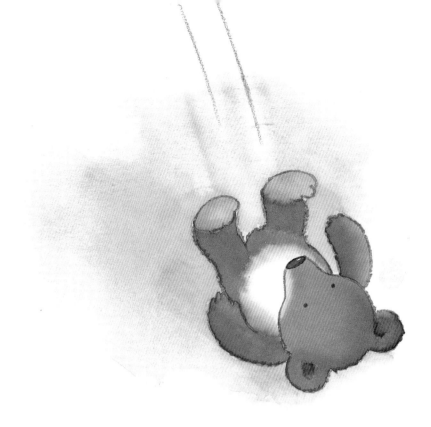

Bear

A small whooshing sound.
Then a plop!
A bounce.
And a kind of squeak.
That was how the bear landed
in my baby sister's playpen.

Have you ever had a bear fall out of the sky, right in front of you?

At first I thought he was a teddy bear. He just lay there, crumpled on the quilt.

Then he got up and took Sophie's drink. And her biscuit. That's when I knew he was real.

The bear climbed out of the playpen and looked at me.

He rolled on his back, lifted his paws and growled.
He seemed to want to play.

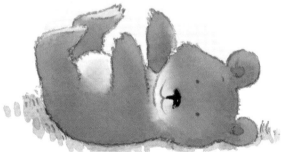

I put him in Sophie's baby bouncer.
He was very good at bouncing, much better than Sophie.

I sneaked the bear into the house under the quilt. At bedtime I hid him among my toys.

'Don't you say anything, Sophie!' I said. 'I want to keep this bear.'

Sophie doesn't say much anyway. She isn't even two yet.

In the morning the sound of shouting
woke me up.

'Sophie, that's naughty!' It was Mum.
She was looking at the feathers.

'Sophie! That's very naughty!'
She was looking at the scribble.

Then she looked at the potty.

'Sophie!' she said. 'Good girl!'

But I don't think it
was Sophie.

I'm sure it wasn't Sophie.
It definitely wasn't
Sophie.

I took the bear to
school in my rucksack.
Everyone wanted to be
my friend.
'Does he bite?' they said.
'He doesn't bite me,'
I said.
'What's his name?'
they said.
'He doesn't
have one.'

We kept him quiet all day
feeding him our lunches. He liked
the peanut butter sandwiches best.

After school my friends came to the house.

'Where is he?' they said.

We played with the bear behind the garage.

We made a
tunnel…

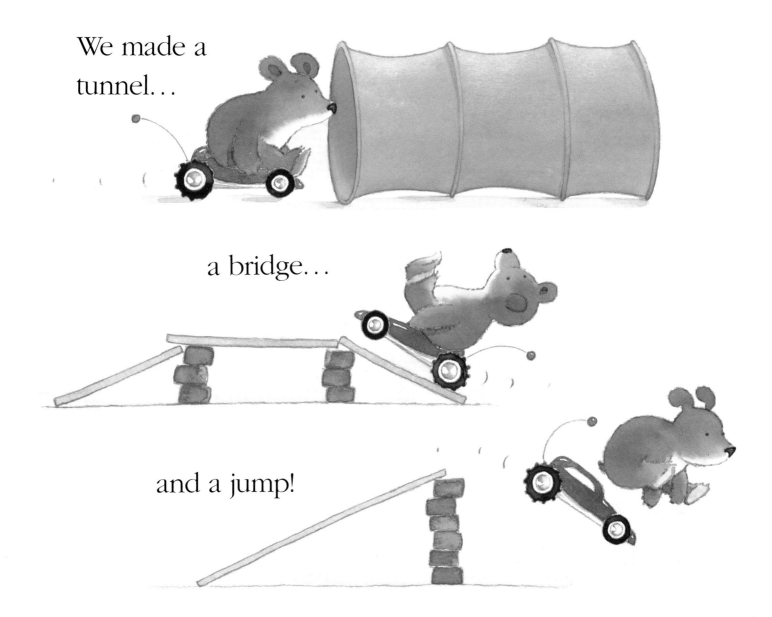

a bridge…

and a jump!

When the car came back the bear
had gone. We looked and looked
but there was no bear anywhere.

At bedtime Sophie
wouldn't go to sleep.

She didn't want her elephant.

She didn't want her rabbit.

She threw them out of the cot.

I gave her my second best pig.

She threw it out.

'Sophie! That's naughty!'
said Mum.

But Sophie just howled.
She wanted the bear.

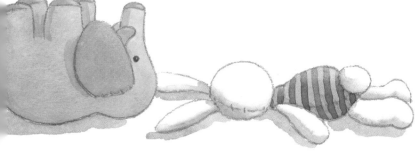

CRASH! BANG!
It was the middle
of the night.
SMASH! CLANG!
The noise was coming from
the kitchen. We crept downstairs
and peeped through the door.
It wasn't a burglar.

'Bear!' said Sophie. 'Naughty!'

So today a serious man in a serious
hat came to look at our bear. He wrote
something in a big black book.

'Will you have to take him away?'
I said.

'We nearly always do,' said the
man. He pointed his pen at my
bear. 'But,' he said, 'this bear is
an Exception.'

'This bear,' he went on, 'has fallen
quite unexpectedly into a storybook.
And it is not up to me to say
what should happen next.'
'So can we keep him?'
I said.

'Ask them,' he said. And he
pointed straight out of the picture
at YOU!

And you thought for a moment.
You looked at the man.
You looked at the bear.
You looked at Sophie.
You looked at me.

And then you said…

'YES YOU CAN!'

So we did.

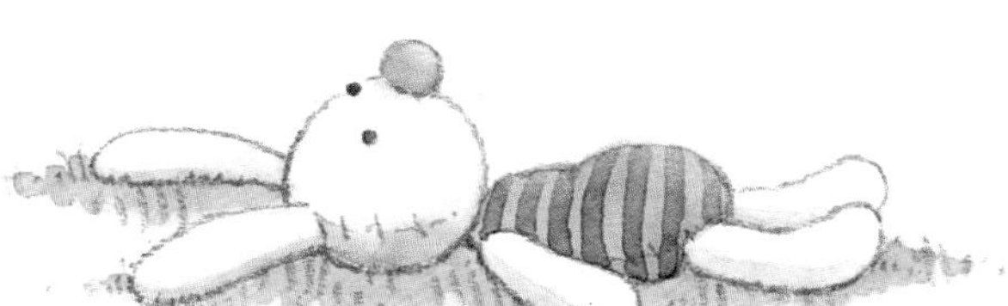

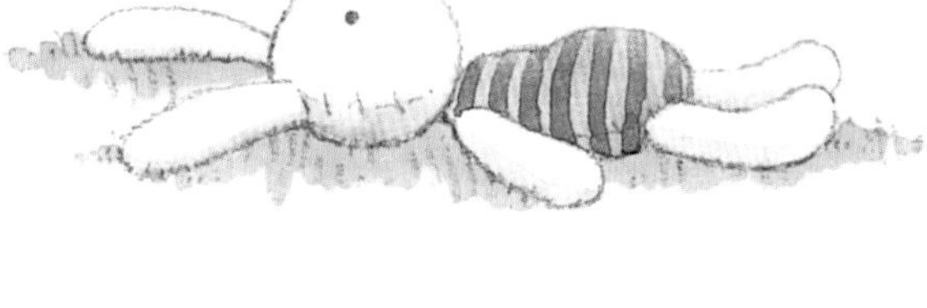